To George, Ben and Frances   SA
For Milly   AA

Published by Caroline House
Boyds Mills Press, Inc.
A Highlights Company
910 Church Street
Honesdale, Pennsylvania 18431
Printed in Hong Kong

Publisher Cataloging-in-Publication Data
Akass, Susan.
Number nine duckling / story by Susan Akass ; pictures by Alex Ayliffe.
—1st U.S. ed.
[32]p. : col. ill. ; cm.
First published 1993 by ABC (All Books for Children), a division of The All
Children's Company Ltd., London.
Summary: A duckling learns he can do anything if he sets his mind to it.
ISBN 1-56397-224-7
[1. Ducks—Fiction.] I. Ayliffe, Alex, ill. II. Title.
[E]—dc20   1993
The Library of Congress Catalog Card Number can be obtained from
the publisher upon request.

The text of this book is set in 16-point Cheltenham.
The illustrations are done in torn paper.
Distributed by St. Martin's Press

10   9   8   7   6   5   4   3   2   1

Number Nine Duckling

Story by SUSAN AKASS

Pictures by ALEX AYLIFFE

BOYDS MILLS PRESS

Delushka Duck was a big white duck with a red face and an orange beak. She was a Russian Muscovy duck, although she had never been to Russia.

Delushka built her nest at the top of a haystack.

"Russian ducks are not silly," she said.
"Other ducks build their nests where foxes
can get them. My nest is fox-proof."
So she sat, keeping her nine large eggs
warm high above the farmyard,
thinking that she was a very
clever duck.
"Nine eggs," she would call
to anyone who would listen,
"and all nine are safe."

At last, one fine spring morning, Delushka heard
a tapping coming from one egg. Suddenly, it cracked
open and there stood a bedraggled yellow duckling.
As Delushka gazed at her proudly, another egg cracked,
and then another and another,
until there were eight
little ducklings clustered
around their mother.

But there was still
one egg in the nest that had
not cracked open. Delushka pecked it.
   "Come on, Number Nine!" she called.
"It's time to hatch."
   A small squeak answered her, and
a few faint taps.

"I will help you," Delushka said loudly,
and pecked sharply on the shell. It cracked
and a very small duckling gazed around dreamily.
"Hurry," said Delushka. "It is time we were off.
There is a lot to do before nightfall." But the
duckling just stood there.

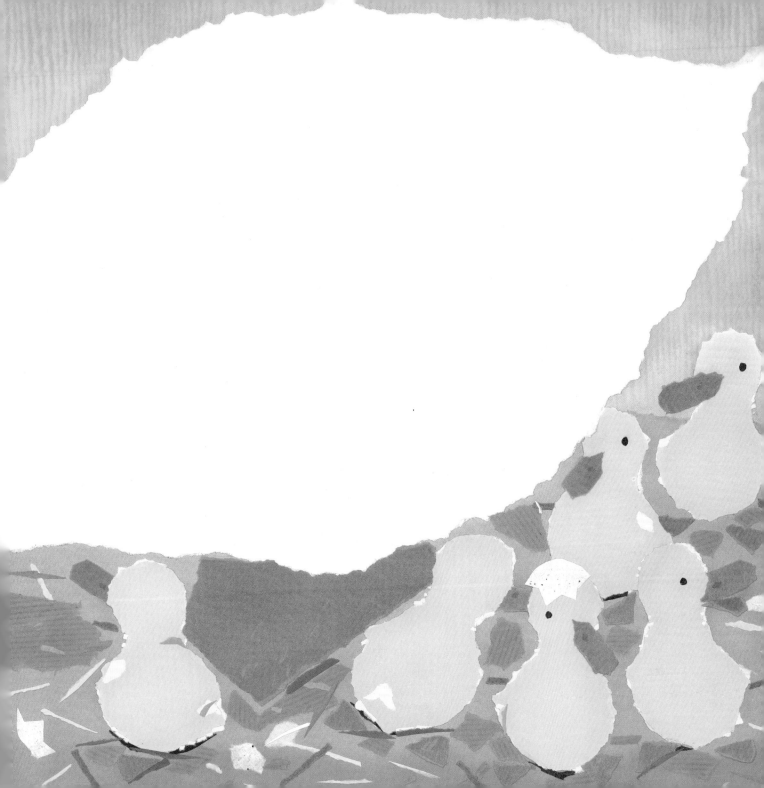

"Breakfast!" Delushka said. "Everyone needs breakfast. Follow me!" And, without a second thought, she soared from the top of the haystack to the ground.

Now, Delushka knew that the nest was high and that her ducklings did not have feathers to fly yet.

But Delushka also knew that they wouldn't stop to think about this. She knew they would follow her.

And she was right. One by one,
they jumped
down,
down,
down,
into the soft grass below them.

And, one by one, they scuttled to Delushka.
Delushka counted as they tumbled,
"One, Two, Three, Four, Five, Six,
Seven, Eight . . . where is Number Nine?"

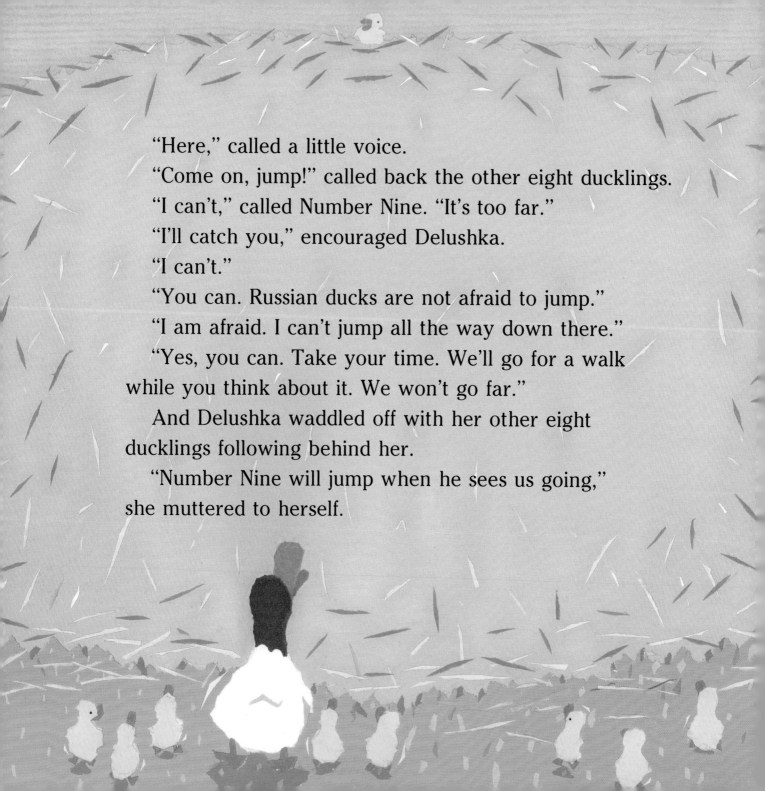

"Here," called a little voice.

"Come on, jump!" called back the other eight ducklings.

"I can't," called Number Nine. "It's too far."

"I'll catch you," encouraged Delushka.

"I can't."

"You can. Russian ducks are not afraid to jump."

"I am afraid. I can't jump all the way down there."

"Yes, you can. Take your time. We'll go for a walk while you think about it. We won't go far."

And Delushka waddled off with her other eight ducklings following behind her.

"Number Nine will jump when he sees us going," she muttered to herself.

But Number Nine did not jump. He watched his mother and brothers and sisters go. He wanted so much to go with them but he could not bring himself to jump.

"I'll close my eyes and jump," he thought.
But then he couldn't move at all.

"I'll try a running start," he thought. But
his legs would not run.

Number Nine sat down and cried.

A sparrow flew by. "What are you doing here all by yourself?" she asked.

"I can't jump," answered Number Nine, tearfully.

"Of course you can," said the sparrow. "Anyone can jump. Watch!" And she did a backwards flip out of the nest and turned two somersaults before bouncing into the grass below.

"See," she called up, "anyone can jump."

"Jump? We can jump!" squealed a brood of yellow chicks. They bobbed up and down like yellow ping-pong balls.

The pony snorted, "Anyone can jump!" and galloped off, bucking and kicking.

"Baaaaa," laughed the lambs. "We're the greatest jumpers!" They bounded away, leaping and twisting.

"It's not that easy when you're as fat as I am," grunted
the pig, "but I'll try." She lumbered up a steep bank.
"One, two, THREE!" and she belly-flopped right into a
muddy puddle. "Huh! Anyone can jump."

Number Nine started to laugh. "I'll try
one little jump right here," he thought.
He sprang up as high as he could.

"That's it," encouraged the pig. "You can jump, too!"

"I can!" cheeped Number Nine and he jumped all over the nest until he reached the edge.

"But I can't jump *down*," he said, sadly.

"Yes, you can," said the pony.
"If you can jump up, you can jump down.
Nothing to it."

"Nothing to it," echoed the lambs
noisily. "Come on, little duck, jump!"

All the other animals joined in the
chant. "Come on, little duck, jump!"

Delushka heard them. She listened
and waddled back to the haystack. She saw
Number Nine teetering on the edge.
"Come on, Number Nine, you can
do it!" she shouted.

Number Nine was so happy to see
his mother that he took a deep breath
and JUMPED into the soft grass at the
bottom of the haystack.

"Anyone can jump!" he cheeped.

Delushka waddled over and gave him a
loving peck. "Now it's time for breakfast
and a swimming lesson," she announced.
"Follow me, everyone!" And she waddled
towards the pond.

"Swimming lesson? I can't swim," said
Number Nine, as he took his place at
the end of the line of ducklings.